For *my* Elliott who has *very* good manners indeed!
S.S.

For Elodie and Rowan who love making a mess
but do so with impeccable manners!
Love, Auntie Ade
A.M.

First published in 2013 by Scholastic Children's Books
Euston House, 24 Eversholt Street, London NW1 1DB
A division of Scholastic Ltd
www.scholastic.co.uk
Associated companies worldwide

Text copyright © 2013 Steve Smallman
Illustrations copyright © 2013 Adria Meserve

PB 978 1407 12181 9

Printed in Singapore
1 2 3 4 5 6 7 8 9 10

TRUMPETY TRUMP!

Written by
Steve Smallman

Illustrated by
Adria Meserve

SCHOLASTIC

Elliott Elephant used to be ... RUDE!

He guzzled his drink and he gobbled his food.

And when he would **trumpet,**
as elephants do,
He'd **trumpety-trump**
from his bottom end too!

He'd frighten the animals close to the ground

By **charging**

and **barging**

and **crashing** around.

He'd **shake** all the monkeys right out of their tree

By **scratching** his bottom too vigorously!

One day the flamingos,
all fluffy and pink,
Were quietly taking
an afternoon drink.

Gentle giraffe took
a delicate sip
As someone decided
to go for a

DIP!

Elliott burst through the trees with a **crash**,
Then **belly-flopped** in with an almighty
sPLASH!

The birds were all soaking —
and so was Giraffe.
And Elliott thought,
"What a jolly good laugh!"

Hippo blew
bubbles out . . .

"Plip plip,
plip plop!"

he liked it so
much that he
just couldn't stop!

Elliott thought
that he'd join
in the game . . .

But sadly his
bubbles were
not quite
the same!

"Shhhh!"
whispered Parrot,
"Please don't make a peep,
At last all my babies
have settled to sleep."

She sat herself down
for a well-deserved rest,

Then Elliott
trum**peted**
under her nest!

The animals shouted,
"Enough is enough!
That Elliott's really
too thoughtless
and rough.

He's rude and he's noisy
and though he's not vicious,
If he's not more careful
he's likely to squish us!"

Then one morning
Elliott terrified Mouse
By plonking a foot through
the roof of his house.

Mouse went bananas
and showing no fear,
He leapt up and grabbed
hold of Elliott's ear!

"Look, what is your problem,
you **big-footed beast?**
Why can't you just watch
where you're going, at least?

Everyone thinks you're a nuisance, you know..."
Then Elliott stared in surprise and said,

"Oh."

"A nuisance?" he sniffled, tears filling his eyes.
"And scary," Mouse added, "because of your size."

"If you were more thoughtful and careful, I'm sure,
We'd all learn to like you an awful lot more!"

So Elliott tried
very hard to be good ...
Stopped charging
and barging
and watched
where he stood.

He tried not to splash and
he tried to be quiet —

And scratch his
behind without
causing a riot.

And what Mouse had told him turned out to be true —
If you care for others they'll care about you.

So Elliott learned how to be a good friend,

Although he still ...

trumpety-trumps
from both ends!